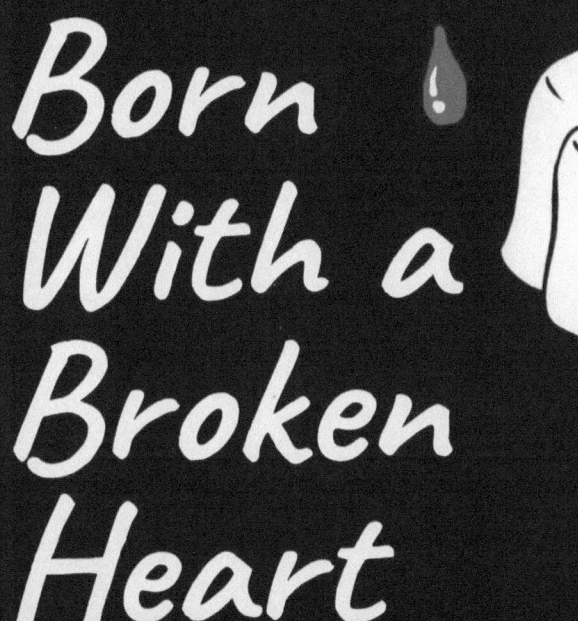

# Born With a Broken Heart

Lauren Michelle Colletti

# Born With a Broken Heart

Lauren Colletti

*Born With a Broken Heart*

Copyright © 2023 by Lauren Colletti

Paperback ISBN: 978-1-63812-806-9
Ebook ISBN: 978-1-63812-807-6

All rights reserved. No part in this book may be produced and transmitted in any form or by any means, electronic, or mechanical, including photocopying, recording, or by any information storage and retrieval system, without permission in writing from the copyright owner.

The viThe views expressed in this work are solely those of the author and do not necessarily reflect the views of the publisher. It hereby disclaims any responsibility for them.

Published by Pen Culture Solutions   09/22/2023

Pen Culture Solutions
1-888-727-7204 (USA)
1-800-950-458 (Australia)
support@penculturesolutions.com

Born With a Broken Heart

Lauren Colletti

In loving memory of Casper, I will miss you every day for the rest of my life.

# Sections

Introduction ..................................................................... 1
I. The Jump ..................................................................... 3
II. The Fall ..................................................................... 47
III. The Land ................................................................. 124

# Introduction

In June 2022 I took a trip to Europe with a friend. It was my first time in Italy/Greece and at the time I was in a very unhappy, dead end, relationship. Unsuspectingly, by July, I was falling in love with an Albanian boy I met in Rome, (while still in my unhealthy partnership). By the time I returned home from my trip, I knew I had to end it for good, despite several attempts, numerous fights and breakups beforehand. I felt stuck and destined to a love life of misery and abuse. Before my 28th birthday on July 15th I ended the dysfunction for once and for all and have stayed out of that toxic, on again off again relationship for good. It was probably one of the best, most liberating decisions I made in my life up until that point.

This book is a collection of thoughts and realizations I've reflected on over the past year. From falling in love in Europe, to getting out of a soul sucking relationship, to having my heart shattered from said long distance situationship, I share poems and excerpts from my broken, healing heart to yours. The last 360 days since I started writing this, my life looks drastically different from any period of time prior. I've since made the decision to also leave my monotonous, unfulfilling 9-5 job and quit living the stereotypical, meaningless and unrewarding mold expected by most Americans. Work a job you hate, get married and have kids by 30, grind out a passionless existence just so one day, hopefully, you get a pension and retire comfortably. Although my life looks incredibly different than how I pictured, I can honestly say although unconventional, my life is now filled with adventure, excitement, joy, magic and a hell of a lot of freedom, connection and wonder. I continue to learn the hard way, but I don't want to call it mistakes because they all turn into humble lessons and opportunities for personal growth.

    I thank you so much for being open to reading my writings and prose, little bits and pieces of memories and stories along my journey. Completely lost, I solo traveled to 6 different countries looking to find something beautiful I eventually saw within myself all along.; independence, wisdom and trust. Born with a broken heart is a story of courage and hope and my wish is to also inspire you to be brave, take a leap of faith and know that no matter where you go, you always have a home to return to, inside yourself.

# I. The Jump

**Tkam Xhan**
I knew it seemed reckless
I knew it was impulsive
I knew the chances of it working were slim to none
I knew it made zero sense
From the outside looking in...
Still when I was with him
I felt something I forgot I could feel,
Alive

**Quando a Roma**
There was something different about his eyes
A thousand miles away
Yet I have never felt more at home

His face
His hugs
His touch
His love
    *- this is what dreams are made of*

**Skin Hunger//Daylight**
I used to only make love in the dark
Concealing parts of me
I didn't wish for others to see
But we made love in the daylight
& I did not hide
I wanted him to have it all
I let him take
Every single part of me

With him, I feel satiated
With you, I felt hungry

How do you tell someone
You are no longer in love with them
Without breaking their soul?
    *- 3 PM confessions*

My appetite for him
His skin
His lips
His touch
I've never been hungrier
    *- Insatiable*

We were timeless
With his sage green eyes
My old soul
& The thrill of his young heart
    - *Where the wild things are*

Because when I was with him
I felt as if I was levitating

The love I dream of is soft like cotton candy. But my heart grew fissures under his hypnotic, canyon eyes. His honeysuckle lips took all my words away. In his presence, I felt helpless. Because he was sweet like bubble gum and my blood sugar was dangerously low.

**Inertia**
I didn't want to fall in love
If he wasn't prepared to catch me
You see,
I didn't wish to fall in love
Because nobody's arms have been strong enough
To keep me from crashing
On the way down

If karma is real, you will find a girl
Who's just like you
But then again
I don't know if you can ever love someone
As much as you love yourself

He thought he was perfect
So no one could be perfect enough for him
  - *You always thought you were too good for me, didn't you?*

To this day
No one has ever gotten to me
The way you did
But he's come
Pretty close

You were a comet
Coming and going so fast
Before I knew it
You were already gone

He touched me like it was the first time
I loved him like it was the last

I lit myself on fire
The moment I fell for you
    *- Guys like you are dangerous*

I watched us slowly fall out of love with
The way petals slowly drift off a rose
One day you look and notice
Everything once beautiful
Has disappeared

Honestly, I still miss you sometimes
But honestly,
Fuck you

I think I could love you forever,
At least I want to...

You will always be a bittersweet memory
    - *Italia*

Nothing scared me more than the thought of forever
But for you, I would try
    *- I think I could love you for the rest of my life*

I forget the exact moment I fell for you
But one day I woke up and realized
I was knee deep in love
And there was no turning back

**Hungry Eyes**
I swear
I could look at nothing but him
For the rest of my life
And never get bored
    *- I guess you could say he was easy on the eyes*

I've never wanted to be in someone's arms
As badly
As I want to be in yours
Right now
    *- 4277 miles*

I told him
I'd rather be poor with you
Than rich with anyone else
    *- I meant it*

He loved me when it was easy
And hated me when it was hard
    *- 10.20 - 7.22*

**Albanian Boy**
I fell into
In his cedar eyes
I haven't been able
To climb my way out since

I would've given him the world if I could've
But I couldn't
So I gave him my heart instead

**Nick**
You had such a fundamental issue
With who I was at the core of my being
& always made sure I knew it
So, for your sake, I hope your next girl
Is the complete opposite of me
I hope she...
1. Loves the gym
2. Comes from wealth
3. Is hyper focused on her appearance
4. Only loves you for your looks
5. Never wants to have sex with you
6. Always pays
7. Measures her food
8. Is forever happy
9. Has zero trauma
10. Stays out late drinking
11. Has no aspirations or dreams
12. Has zero student loans/debt
13. Doesn't want to get married until she's 35 or have kids until she's 40
14. Is free of baggage
15. Doesn't care if you spend time with her
16. Loves BMWS, Florida, and Bitcoin
17. Doesn't have any wants or needs

And I hope your picture-perfect Barbie doll is such a mirror-spitting image of you that one day you grow to resent her.

Because then you'll realize it wasn't me you hated so much, it was yourself.

I thought you would show me what love was
Instead, you showed me what it's not

I never did cocaine
But you were the closest thing to it

They call it young love
But with you I wanted to grow old

**Fleetwood Road**
As I drove by
The road I'd mindlessly drive past
Every day for two years
I thought to myself
Isn't it funny how we never know
It's the last time
Until after it's gone?

**Jardin**
I can't help
But lose my composure
Whenever you come around

His heart was so dark
yet he was the brightest thing I'd ever seen
    - *awestruck*

Falling for him
Was jumping into quicksand

**Halloween in Commack**
I hate to break it to you
But just as you made me fall in love with you
You also made me
Fall out of love with you
You were the reason we collapsed
& you have yourself to thank

**N.C**
I saw your greatness
But all you saw was my weakness

**The Ex Files**
So, go on
And tell them
How you did everything right
& How I did you so wrong
But don't forget to tell them
How you broke my heart, soul & mind
Because what you forgot to mention is how
You left me no choice but to leave you
You backed me up
Against a wall
Then cried that I hurt you
In the process of trying to save myself

**West Palm Beach**
I've lost friends over you
I've lost my pride
I've lost sleep and self-respect
But I won't lose another ounce of dignity
Over you ever again

It's not that I didn't trust men
It's that I didn't trust myself
To love the right ones

**Flor**
He was sweet like bourbon
But went down like moonshine

# II. The Fall

**Born with A Broken Heart**
I never remember a time in my life that I didn't feel sad
Even in my happiest moments
I'd grieved that they would soon be over
Even when I felt the most love
I feared the loss that would someday come
Even while I was up so high
I worried about when I'd come crashing down
I never can recall a time in my life
When I didn't hurt
It's as if I was born
With a broken heart

**Cold front**
We were hot like August
He was warm like May
But leaving him in June
I've never felt colder

I gave my love freely
To the wrong people
In the end
I paid a heavy price
    *- It cost me everything*

**Betrayed**
It's not only lovers
Who hold the potential
To break your heart
It's the women you trusted
The ones you called sisters
Who carry the sharpest knives
Stabbing you in the back
While smiling to your face
    *- I've lost a lot of fake friends this year*

If people tell me I'm so good
Then why do they treat me
So bad?
    *- Crying on my birthday*

It seems I only give people my heart
If they're guaranteed to break it

**Butterfingers**
I handed him my heart
But he didn't know how to hold it

I was in love with you
You were in lust with me

Not being with you
Is gnawing away at my heart
     - *LDR*

I suppose I've always dreamt of a reciprocal love. One where they fell for me as hard as I fell for them. Because my heart doesn't know how to not get its hopes up. My heart doesn't understand how to avoid disappointment. So here I am again, giving somebody my all, going the extra mile, when they won't even give me an inch.
    *- distended*

I couldn't care more
He couldn't care less

He was all that I wanted
& all that I couldn't have

**Amorphous**
I need to stop handing my heart
To people who never asked for it in the first place
Because I give my love to people
Who don't know what to do with it
& so they carry my heart
But not the responsibility to hold it

How is it
No matter how many people
Have come after you
You're still always there
Lurking
In the back of my mind?
    *- Will I ever stop dreaming of you?*

Some days I can't get you out of my head
*Today is one of them*

It's not the bad boys
We need to watch out for
It's the ones who play nice
    *- Let's call a spade a spade*

I wanted you throughout all of your seasons
Your winter, spring, summer, and fall
But you only wanted my summer
And nothing more

They all wanted my naked body
But none of them my naked soul

I guess all you will ever be
Is a mesmerizing fantasy
      *- Trevi*

Letting go of you
While I'm still in love with you
Feels like throwing my heart
Into a blender
⁃ 9.22

You wouldn't allow
Anyone into your heart
I'm not sure why I thought
I'd be the exception

**R.S**
You were only supposed to be temporary
But you felt permanent
And now I'm homesick
Without you here

Why do I only give my time
To those who are bound
To waste it?

I used sex to numb the pain
But the next day wake up
Feeling the same
    *- If not worse*

I let them in my body
I let them in my bed
Won't let them in my heart
Can't let them in my head

You cared more about being right
Than you did losing me
So congratulations
You've earned your pride
And lost me
    *- I hope it was worth it*

Losing you wasn't supposed to be this hard
After all,
You were never really mine
To begin with

I never got to fully love you
The way I wanted
& that's what hurts the most

My heart hemorrhaged
The moment you left

Helplessness is realizing
That absolutely nothing
Will make you feel better
Except for them

**Gelato Italiano**
He had hazel eyes and rustic hair
A soft smile and gentle hands
He'd seen too much at an early age
His heart had been broken
By people who claimed to always be there

So he built up walls
No one could tear down
Sworn off everyone
In his town
And then I came around...

His touch was a force
Yet comforting, all the same,
I let down my guard
Whenever he said my name

He was sweet, and he was kind
With a generous side

Until he wasn't...

We got into our first argument
And I saw his temper
Something I can't forget
And I'll always remember

He yelled that he hated me
But then that he loved me
He said he was sorry
But made sure I knew he was above me

I told myself I'd never be with
Someone who spits words
That can not be undone nor fixed

Someone who changes
At the flip of a dime
That day I made a choice
I'd not dare give him more time

So to the breathtaking boy
With the dreamy eyes
I hope you know
This KILLS ME inside

Because as much as I want you
It's something I must do
You've shown me your true colors
And they aren't blue

They're black they're gray
They're dark as night
Your brightness flickers out
As soon as we fight

So I'm letting you go
As hard as it is
I wish the best in life for you kid

Just know I'm not doing this
Because I don't share
Love for you, not at all
Its because for once I must care
About myself more
And trust me I swear
It breaks me in half to cut these ties
But because I choose me

I'm saying goodbye …

**Chasing Boys III**
I flew to the Heartbreaker boys
The way moths do to a flame
Seeking light and warmth
Only to get torched

How many more loves
Do I need to lose
Before I find one
I get to keep?

The problem wasn't that I hated him
But that it might be easier if I did

They told me to love
As if I had never been hurt
So I did
And all I have to show for it
Are these holes
In my heart

It's easy to find nice guys
It's harder to find ones
That stay that way

I overlooked them treating me with hatred
And calling it love
Because I wanted to believe
That someone could love me

**Daddy Issues**
Sometimes I wonder
If I would still want them
If they wanted me as badly, back

I've met a lot of men who want me
But none who actually love me

I got you
You got to me
That's it
   *- the end*

Some use drugs
Some use sex
Some use rock and roll
But bad boys
Have always been my vice

I wasn't ready to stop loving you

He stole my breath away
So now that he's gone
I can't breathe

I'm tired of letting people in
Just to be let down
I don't want to get close to someone
Only to be left alone
Right back where I started
More empty and numb
Than the time before

I always gave them my heart
They never gave theirs back

**Zan**
That young love kind of feeling
When you jump off the deep end
And I was really sinking
While I thought that I was floating...

Then you came round and tricked me
When I thought you had picked me
Now I feel fucking silly
Cause I hoped we could really
Be

& little boy
You could've grown up
To be a man that I had loved
Oh little boy
You really swept me up

I guess what they say is true
That love is blind
Because so I am
For ignoring all the red flags
So little boy
All I can say is that
I pray one day you turn into a man

& I could've loved you right
But you're not ready
Cause you pose as a man
Hiding behind
A scared little boy

He was hot like July
But cold like December

His eyes changed in the sunlight
His temper did by moonlight

I knew you would only break my heart
Even still, I loved you anyway

**Alone in Portugal**
Here I am now
Living out the life
I told you I always wanted
But now you're not here
So I guess,
I didn't get everything I'd dreamed
After all...

You refused to believe
Anyone could ever love you
So when I tried
You pushed me away
& left me with no choice but to leave
So when you claim nobody will ever love you
Remember, you did this to yourself
    *- I never wanted this*

I wanted you old
I wanted you poor
I wanted you sick
I wanted your highs
I wanted your lows
I wanted your happy days
I wanted your sad days
I wanted your good
I wanted your bad
I wanted your in between
Fuck, I just wanted you
    *- but you didn't want me back*

**Tindering**
5, 10, 20 other guys
Just to try and forget one
　　*- It's not working*

**Flight to Madrid**
Ignorance truly is bliss
I was so naive when it came to loving you
Blinded by your light
Closing my eyes to your darkness
I couldn't see the truth
Turning red flags into a rainbow
Warning signs became excuses
Nothing could convince my heart
Of what it didn't want to know
So, I crashed coming down from the clouds
Because as they say
It's not the fall that kills you
But the landing

I wish these feelings
Left as easily as you did

You never did quite look at me
The way I looked at you
    *- Love is blinding*

My heart is a graveyard
Of people I tried to love
My heart is a graveyard
Of all the times
I've died in the process

**Heartsick**
I know you didn't want to fall for him
But you tripped
& now you don't know how to get up
I know you tried to make him home
But he was never up for sale

You put me through hell
So why did you feel like heaven?

He was a cut
That never quite healed

You didn't make a fool of me
I made a fool of myself
Trying to earn love
From someone
Who had none to give

**Emily in Paris, Lauren in Greece**
I tried to leave the loneliness
But it followed wherever I went

I'd rather you have broken my heart
All at once
Rather than over and over again
Because now it's shattered into pieces
And I don't know how to put it back together

I've been
Running
And running
After you
And honestly
My feet fucking hurt
    *- you only wanted to be chased but never caught*

I wanted you for eternity
You only wanted me for a moment

I want someone
To look at me
The same way
I look at you

All I ever wanted
Was for the person I chose
To choose me back
    *- I guess that's too much to ask*

Of them all
You're the most disappointing dream
To never come true

We were long gone
But I didn't want to pull
The life support

I was so high on your lust, I mistook it for love

**Stories of Self Hatred**
I get stared at by day
Messages flood my inbox by night
I'm honked at when I go for a run
& when I swipe right, they all swipe back
I don't mean to sound conceited
But I'm told I'm pretty all the time
And I can't help but think
What a waste my youth has been
When I've spent it
Preoccupied with looking good
Losing weight, poisoning myself
Crawling in my skin, fighting to stay relevant
How useless it is
To be beautiful
When you're misunderstood
Unloved
And alone

**Lazio**
Here we were
Finally in the same city
Yet you've never felt
Farther away

I pulled an all nighter
Our first day together
I remember we talked till 6 AM
About the places we would go
Toyko, Paris,
I'd show you my city
You'd show me yours
Now I wait
Up all night
For a text that never comes
While you spend the night
With somebody else in your arms
    *- That used to be me*

What a convincing illusion you were...

**Chasing Boys IV**
Danny had gray eyes and an intimidating demeanor
His mom from Colombia and his dad Italian
With tattoos up his neck but a gentle smile
I fell for him the first night we met
Nick had piercing blue eyes and soft black hair
His arms fit perfectly around my waist
His kiss tasted like whiskey
And in the heat of the summer, I fell by the next day
Ram couldn't care less about anything
So when he took interest in me, I thought it meant something
His eyes were green but unpredictable
I didn't fall for him right away
But once I did, my heart never knew such a longing
He was mostly sour but sometimes sweet
I was madly in love after only 10 days
Pablo was a modest boy from Colombia
His lips looked like sugar and I wanted a taste
His hazel eyes seemed lost but kind
He made me laugh and yearn to be touched
I fell for him after only one shot
I collected boys that loved to run
Each different than the next, yet all the same
I chased and I fell, I fell and I chased
Losing them all
I caught none, along the way

# III. The Land

It takes time
But if you loved once
You can love again
    *- don't let heartbreak fool you*

If you don't love yourself
You'll never believe
When another person says they do
    · *this, I've learned the hard way*

Your self-hatred is not your own
Self-hatred is inherited
It says
"People would love you
If only you were pretty enough
They wouldn't have left
Had you been thin enough"
Self-hatred is passed down
It is built
Brick by brick
Handed to us by people
Who really just hated themselves

She spoke
For years
She yelled
But kept her fingers
Pressed to her ears
She screamed
She begged
She ignored
She fell ill
She grew old
She became tired
She asked to be heard
She's finally ready to listen
    *- intuition*

Love
Shouldn't
Feel
Like
An
Obstacle
Course

I wish the healing
Came as quickly
As the aching

I was once so afraid
Of losing you
Now my only fear
Is losing more of myself
By staying
    *- Barren*

I look forward to nothing more
Than the day I leave
And never look back
    - *So long, Long Island*

**A Love Story**
I don't care if I'm the most beautiful girl in the world
As long as I'm the most beautiful girl to you
    *- She says to herself in the mirror*

**Gypsy Heart**
I've spent my life
A lone wanderer
My gypsy heart would allow me to get
Only so comfortable
Until it was time
To pack up and leave
Because I felt safer barricading walls
Hiding away in my caravan
Than to stay put
& let someone actually love me
Running from house to house
Looking for someone
To call home

I'd rather be alone
For the rest of my life
Than settle
For someone who doesn't know
How to treat me
Ever again
    *- 07.22*

When you're that lonely
You begin to confuse attention
For love

It's okay to miss someone
But not want them back
    - *Tropism*

It's OK to miss someone
& sometimes, want them back
   - *Stasis*

He told me what I could and couldn't do
Where I could and couldn't go
What I could and couldn't wear
Who I could and couldn't speak to
How I could and couldn't think
He told me what I could and couldn't be
In order to be loved by him
So I did myself a favor
And loved myself more
I let go of him
And chose myself instead
    *- Now I couldn't care less*

The only thing wrong with you
Is the way you have been loved
    *- You are not damaged*

The scariest thing about abusive people
Isn't the abuse itself
It's the image they paint for others
Making everyone around you think
What a standup person they are
Everyone's convinced they're so great
So they doubt your story
And believe the abuser instead
    *- Smear campaign*

**Sanctuary**

I no longer crave a love that feels like insomnia
My soul craves a love that feels like rest

It's not that you're unlovable
It's that you've been loving people
Who don't know how to properly love you
    - *Note to self*

I'm tired of teaching boys
How to treat a woman
I'm sick of them experimenting
What not to do through me
It's not my job to raise a boy
To show him how to properly love a woman
Trial and error
One test run after the next
I get the worst of them
Only for them to give their best
To somebody else
I need to be with someone
Who doesn't need to learn how to be a man
Because they already are one
    *- Not your project*

I wouldn't say you were a mistake
But a painful & necessary lesson

I didn't leave because I didn't love you
I left because for once
I had to love me

Never sacrifice yourself
To keep a man
It's better to lose him
Than it is yourself

I would run back to the boy who broke me
Just to rid the pain of losing him
Only for him to break me & lose him again
    *- Feel the pain now or feel the pain later*

Isn't it interesting how we fall out of love
With the person whose no good for us
The moment we fall in love with ourselves instead
   *- out of love with you, in love with me*

It took me 4 years
To heal from a relationship
That was only 2
Stop putting a due date on your healing
It'll only take longer
There is nothing wrong with you
If you can't "get over" something
In a certain amount of time
When we judge our process, we delay it
If we broke our leg
We wouldn't feel like a failure
If it took longer to heal than expected
We should do the same when it comes to our hearts
    *- Healing doesn't have a timeline*

He refused to see my worth
So I left him
& found it in myself

I decided to stop searching for the man of my dreams
& become the woman of my dreams
Instead

When they list off all the reasons they love me
I want "she's beautiful"
To be the very last one
    *- Beauty is only skin deep*

If they're not the one
There's nothing you can do to make them it
No matter how badly you want them to be
    *- Still learning*

The life you dream
Is on the other side of those uncomfortable decisions
You've been putting off
    - *Espana*

What you're seeking outside
Is a reflection of what you're needing
Inside

**My Last Relationship Taught Me**
Control and love are not the same

You shouldn't have to beg for attention

Self-sacrifice is not the same as compromise

You only attract people who are highly critical of you because you are highly critical of yourself

Sexual incompatibility is a valid reason to leave

A man won't be scared away but a boy will

If they tell you you're too much tell them to go find less

Someone who truly loves you won't want to change you

A dysfunctional person will shame you for your flaws, a conscious person will support you

You won't have to chase what's meant for you

You deserve to be heard

It's OK for someone to disagree with you, it's not OK for someone to invalidate or gaslight you

Just because they reject you doesn't mean you should reject yourself

Abuse is never justifiable

You shouldn't have to abandon yourself to keep someone

You're not selfish for wanting to feel wanted

It is not your job to rescue them

You will not have to fight for the right persons love

It is better to be lonely alone than lonely with someone who claims to love you

If they won't choose you choose yourself and walk away

Breaking up and getting back together is toxic

Your partner shouldn't make you feel like something is wrong with you

Your partner should feel like your lover, not your parent

You won't have to negotiate who you are for the right person

It's not on you to love the demons out of someone

Their inability to love you properly is not a personal failure

Date someone who sees your worth, not someone you have to prove it to

You deserve love, you don't need to earn it

Stop enduring pain and calling it love

If they recreate your trauma, it's a trauma bond, not love

Healthy love will help you find yourself not lose yourself

Find someone who treats you as their equal not inferior

Your person will integrate your wounds not exacerbate them

A safe person will help you trust yourself not doubt yourself

Someone being your best friend is not enough reason to stay together

Love isn't enough to make a relationship last

You need respect, not a companion

The weight of the relationship should not fall on one person
A relationship is a mutual, equal effort

Just because they are a good person doesn't mean they're good for you

**To the Heartbroken Girl**
I know he made you lose your composure whenever he came around
I know you could stare into his eyes all night
And that your favorite thing to do was forget the world while he was lying next to you
I know his touch gave you goosebumps
And that the thought of eternity scared the hell out of you
But when you thought of forever with him you were never less afraid
I know he was the brightest star you'd ever seen in the sky
And you would follow him anywhere he wanted to go
I know you tried to love the darkness out of him
To open his heart
Because you convinced yourself his love was all you'd ever need
I know he appeared to be an angel but oh, how he put you through hell
I know his words cut like a knife
And you told yourself that if only you were good enough
THEN he would choose you
I know you blame yourself for him not being able to see you
And how some nights you were right in front of him
But never felt so invisible
I know you recoil at the thought of losing him
But my dear he was never yours to begin with
I know he feels like a wound that could never quite heal
But I want you to remember
That you deserve to be somebody's first choice
Not an option when they get lonely
You deserve someone who is in love with you
Not someone who says they love you yet treats you as if you don't exist

You are worthy of someone
Who looks at you the same way you look at them
I know it seems like your heart is going to burst open
And they are all there is
I know how bad it hurts but you can't receive love
From someone who has none to give
You can't feel whole
While being with someone who makes you feel empty
I know my love because I've been there
I know because I feel it too
    *- Heartbroken girl, I am you*

**To the Girl Who is Hurting**
I see the tears in your eyes
I know you worry everyone's doubts about you were right
And you were wrong to think you could believe in yourself
Because your entire life people have told you, you can't
But most of all, you more than anyone else
You see, I know you don't think you're anything special
I hear you cry at night, wondering why you lose everyone you love
You feel you're not worthy of happiness
You tell yourself joy is for other people, everyone but you
Because you doubt you deserve anything substantial
You allow broken men into your heart... you try to fix them with your kindness
When you ultimately realize you can't change anybody no matter how good you are
You tell yourself you couldn't save him because YOU are too damaged
I know the silence kills you... I know you feel all alone in this world
Like you could disappear, and no one would even know
I know how disappointed you feel when you look in the mirror
You've convinced yourself you're too flawed to love
I know some days your heart feels so heavy it's going to fall out your chest
I know you care so much, sometimes, you wish you didn't care at all
I know you don't know how to stop missing him...
Because you look for love in all the wrong places
You ask yourself what's wrong with you
Why you can't seem to find what it is you are looking for
But what is it, exactly? That you are looking for?
You see, I think you settle for the bare minimum

Because you've never seen to believe that you can
But my dear girl, you can trust yourself
You can let go… it's OK to say goodbye to the person you gave your heart to
That doesn't give you anything in return
I know you feel it all; I know how dark it gets
You carry the weight of the world on your shoulders
But I promise you, this sadness you are feeling
Some days it will engulf you; some nights you feel like you are drowning
Life can really feel like treading water
You can hardly stay afloat
But I swear, you'll look back and be so proud
That when you felt like sinking, that's how you learned to swim

**New Years Day**
You knew... You knew the last time you saw him would be the final time
Since you can't forget, no matter how badly you want to, the way he made you feel
And that's what killed the most
To know how hooked you became
On the idea of him loving you
So, when he didn't, you split open
But he never did see you the way you saw him
You wish your feelings would go as easily as him
Because you knew he would break my heart
Yet still, you loved him anyway
But darling, never stop loving
Let go of what doesn't want to be kept
Say goodbye to anybody who doesn't look at you
Like the masterpiece you are
And just you watch
One day, it'll be your turn
To receive back all the love that you give
And on that day, you will be so grateful
It didn't work out with anyone else

**No Dejes de Amar**
You wish you could stop
Since nothing has shattered you as much as love
No matter how many times you've had your heartbroken
You still do
And I know you want to turn it off
Because it seems like everyone has found their person except you
You doubt they're out there
That you'll ever get your turn
But baby girl
I don't want you to give up
Keep loving
It takes no courage to put up walls
You have so much love to give
And you might feel lonely but with that you are brave
I know it doesn't seem worth it
To give someone your all for nothing
But my dear, you did the strongest thing a person could do
You loved

**To The Girl Who is Lonely**
I'd rather you be lonely without than lonely with
Because I know it stings in his absence
But need I remind you how much it burned in his presence
I know it seems your heart is an emotional rehab for wounded men
Yet you can never quite get them to heal
You end up having to mend yourself together after tirelessly trying to fix them
You let people into your bed
Because you want to remember what it's like to be held
Your skin hungers to be touched
But when they don't call the next day
You remember how empty you feel
When he texts you at 2 in the morning
You accept the crumbs he throws your way
Because you tell yourself it's better than none at all
But you don't know how rare you are
So don't be accessible to those who don't see your value
Let your silence be a consequence to those who don't celebrate your worth
I know you feel fragmented
But darling
You were born whole
How could you not be loved
When you are love itself?

**Not on the Dollar Menu**
He sunk his teeth into my flesh
Biting my neck, licking his fingers
He told me my skin tasted sweet
And indeed, his lips did hit the spot
But he consumed me like he hadn't eaten in days...
I don't want to be somebody's quick fix
A drive-through, fast food, easy way out
Because they only call when they're starving
But go as soon as they finish
And after they're done ... well, they never want seconds
I need someone who won't leave after they've had their fill
I want someone who doesn't desire solely my breasts, legs, and thighs
But all of me
Someone who comes back time and time again
I crave someone whose not hungry nor half empty
But somebody
Whose already full
 *- Baby, I'm fine dining*

I blocked you not because I didn't want you
I blocked you because for once
I needed to want me more

Thank you for breaking my heart
Because the love I was trying to give you
I learned to give myself

One of the hardest lessons in life,
Learning to let go of what doesn't wish to be kept

You deserve to be more
Than somebody's sometimes
You deserve more
Than the bare minimum

We endure pain
And call it love

Losing someone you love is hard
Losing yourself is harder

Find someone
Who knows everything you hate about yourself
And loves it
Anyway

Find someone
Who makes you love yourself more
Not less

Love is a practice, not a word

Don't confuse them wanting
To love you for the night
For them actually
Wanting to love you

Before I die
All I want is to know
What it's like to love
And be loved in return
I guess I'll have to find out with myself

Dear 2023,
I pray you are the year
I stop trying to give my love
To people who want it the least

I hope you understand
But I had to say goodbye to you
To say hello to me

Baby girl,
If he hides you
He's not it

Loving an abusive person harder
Won't make them stop abusing
    *- set ~~them~~ yourself free*

The moment I was ready to love myself
Was the moment I was ready
To stop loving you

The first step towards finding the man of your dreams,
Is to let go of the boy

Find someone who looks at you like the North Star
No matter how many others there are in the sky
You're the only one they see

The problem isn't that you're not enough
The problem is, you don't see that you are

This generation has it all wrong
Your worth can't be measured by an algorithm
Your value doesn't come from
How many likes you get
Being special isn't dependent on your reach
What matters can't be seen by a follower count

When I looked for a home
In other people
My heart always felt
Homeless

I held onto you
For fear that I'd miss you
Turns out in the end
The only one I missed
Was myself
    *- I had to lose you to (re)find me*

NEVER beg someone to not leave you
If they want to go
Show them to the fucking door

I loved him the way
I wanted someone to love me
With an unwavering, fervor
An unconditional devotion
Now the work
Was pouring that same commitment
Into myself

Never question your lovability
Because of someone's inability to love you

If you have to beg for their attention
You shouldn't even want it to begin with

The simple solution for someone saying
They are too busy?
Find someone who isn't.
We make time for things we care about
As long as you're not a priority, they'll always find an excuse

**Not Your Toy**
I'm more than just the girl you call when you have nothing better to do
Or someone you use to pass time, to text when you're bored or feeling lonely
I'm not a placeholder here to boost your ego
Until something better comes along
You hit me up only to feed your pride
To make sure I still want you, that I'm still there
You disappear for days and weeks on end
But circle back when I start to move on
Giving just enough but never your all
I'm more than someone to feed you attention
I'm more than just an option
Cause if I'm not your everything
I don't want to be anything at all
    *- I deserve more than the crumbs you throw my way*

Note to my 27-year-old self:
If they make you feel unwanted
They don't want you
Go find someone who does

www.ingramcontent.com/pod-product-compliance
Lightning Source LLC
LaVergne TN
LVHW091545060526
838200LV00036B/708